We Can Be Responsible!

WE GET DRESSED

By Lynda Arnéz

Gareth Stevens
PUBLISHING

Please visit our website, www.garethstevens.com. For a free color catalog of all our high-quality books, call toll free 1-800-542-2595 or fax 1-877-542-2596.

Cataloging-in-Publication Data

Names: Arnéz, Lynda.
Title: We get dressed / Lynda Arnéz.
Description: New York : Gareth Stevens Publishing, 2020. | Series: We can be responsible!
Identifiers: ISBN 9781538239070 (pbk.) | ISBN 9781538239094 (library bound) | ISBN 9781538239087 (6 pack)
Subjects: LCSH: Clothing and dress–Juvenile literature.
Classification: LCC TX340.A76 2019 | DDC 391–dc23

First Edition

Published in 2020 by
Gareth Stevens Publishing
111 East 14th Street, Suite 349
New York, NY 10003

Editor: Kristen Nelson
Designer: Sarah Liddell

Photo credits: Cover, p. 1 Monkey Business Images/Shutterstock.com; p. 5 Lopolo/Shutterstock.com; p. 7 Africa Studio/Shutterstock.com; p. 9 Iakov Filimonov/Shutterstock.com; p. 11 Westend61/Getty Images; pp. 13, 24 (skirt) George Rudy/Shutterstock.com; pp. 15, 24 (hat) Olga Enger/Shutterstock.com; pp. 17, 24 (socks) Sean Justice/Photodisc/Getty images; p. 19 Mike Kemp/Getty Images; p. 21 JGI/Jamie Grill/Getty Images; p. 23 Sergey Novikov/Shutterstock.com.

Printed in the United States of America

CPSIA compliance information: Batch #CS19GS: For further information contact Gareth Stevens, New York, New York at 1-800-542-2595.

Contents

We are going to the park!
Let's get dressed!

Raya likes to pick out her clothes.

Judy wants her mom to help.

Kelvin chooses
a blue shirt.
He buttons it himself!

Elyse and Gemma
put on skirts.

It is sunny out.
We will wear hats
to the park!

Riley wants to run
in the park.
She puts socks and
sneakers on.

Lara puts on her dad's shoes.
They are too big!

Ernest ties his shoes.
He is ready to go!

You can get dressed, too!
What will you wear?

Words to Know

hat

skirt

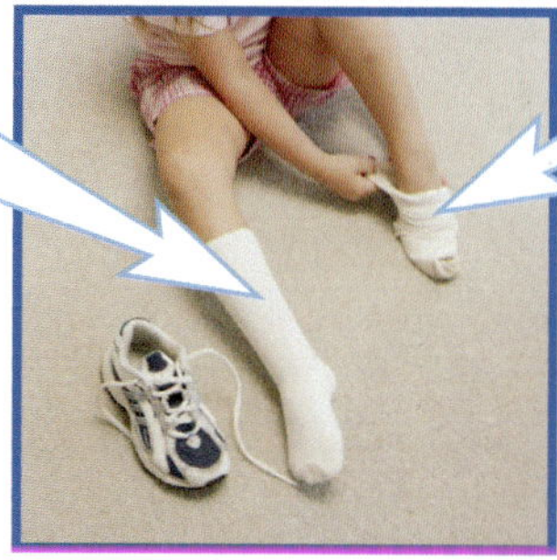

socks

Index